MALAY FOLKLORE
A Contemporary Retelling

MALAY FOLKLORE
A Contemporary Retelling

D Ruse

ATHENA PRESS
LONDON

MALAY FOLKLORE
A Contemporary Retelling
Copyright © D Ruse 2007

All Rights Reserved

No part of this book may be reproduced in any form
by photocopying or by any electronic or mechanical means,
including information storage or retrieval systems,
without permission in writing from both the copyright
owner and the publisher of this book.

ISBN 10-digit: 1 84401 953 5
ISBN 13-digit: 978 1 84401 953 3

First Published 2007 by
ATHENA PRESS
Queen's House, 2 Holly Road
Twickenham TW1 4EG
United Kingdom

Printed for Athena Press

Preface

THE Malay belt in South-East Asia comprises the islands of Indonesia; the oil sultanate of Brunei; the city state of Singapore; and, last but not least, its northern neighbour Malaysia, the Florida-like appendage at the tip of the South-East Asian land mass. The Malaysian states of Sarawak and Sabah are on the island of Borneo, where the sultanate of Brunei is. Like any other culture, Malays have their own folklore, a legacy of tales told by the elderly in kampungs[1] that have been transmitted throughout the ages without any need to check on their historical truth or to separate myth from fact.

Malays have their rich tapestry of folklore and legends woven around witches, princes and princesses, ghouls, damsels in distress and even inanimate objects such as stones and mountains. The following ten selected stories have been passed down through ancient oral tradition and most Malays would be familiar with these largely improbable tales.

To preserve this folklore for posterity, and to give it a more contemporary setting in line with modern times and globalisation, we present Malay Folklore: a Contemporary Retelling, a tongue-in-cheek version that is certain to stir a little nostalgia among many Malays, and perhaps provoke a little consternation from the more puritan who would not countenance any retelling that does not conform to what they deem to be culturally appropriate.

The contemporary version of these age-old stories has a twofold purpose: to remind Malays, especially the tech-savvy youth, of this legacy that is part and parcel of the Malay oral tradition, and also to bring a modern touch to tales which are worn out over time, and are becoming irrelevant to many Malays. Technology and Westernised education have conspired to make Malay folklore a forgotten piece of the Malay cultural fibre; hence this

---

[1] The word for 'villages' in Malay.

Preface

attempt to keep it from disappearing altogether in a world where old is oftentimes regarded as passé.

Since this retelling is in English, there are bound to be semantic errors and some factual inaccuracies, for which we humbly apologise. However, as to the contemporary aspect of the retelling, no apology is offered, since folklore, by its very nature, is an oral tradition of the Malays that is mired in ambiguity and has certainly seen its original veracity stretched to the limits as the story gets told and retold throughout the ages.

Contents

Batu Belah, Batu Bertangkup	9
Second take	13
Bawang Putih, Bawang Merah	15
Second take	19
Puteri Gunung Ledang	21
Second take	25
Raja Bersiong	27
Second take	31
Si Tanggang	33
Second take	37
Pak Pandir	39
Second take	42
Si Luncai	45
Second take	48
Badang	49
Second take	53
Angan Angan Mat Jenin	55
Second take	58
Singapura Di Langgar Todak	59
Second take	63
Postscript	65

Batu Belah, Batu Bertangkup

Batu Belah, Batu Bertangkup
(Split Rock, Conjoined Rock)

A WIDOW and her two children lived on the fringes of the jungle. Eking out a living from the nearby river, the widow would leave the two children at home by themselves, trusting her daughter to look after her younger brother while she went out to catch fish.

One night, she had a dream and started to crave for the roe of a *tembakul* fish. Day upon day she scoured the river, trying to catch a *tembakul* fish with roe, but to no avail. Until one fine day, her net found the desired catch. Ecstatic beyond words, she brought home the fish, cooked it and left it in a basket suspended high above the floor. Before going out to visit her husband's grave, she left this important message to her daughter:

> You and your brother can eat the fish, but leave the roe for me.

After she had left the house, the son woke up hungry and cried for food. His sister gave him rice and a piece of fish with some of the roe. Not satisfied, her brother cried for more. He particularly wanted the roe. The sister obliged and pulled the basket down, but chided him for wanting more, asking that some be left for their mother. Without warning, the boy seized all the roe and dashed off, eating it all in a corner of the house. The sister was really scared, as she knew they would be in trouble, so decided to fry some fish as replacement for the roe.

Soon thereafter, the widow came home, and asked her daughter to bring her some rice and roe. When only fish was served, she asked for the roe, only to be told that her little son had eaten it all. Despondent and highly distraught, she cried, 'I told you to keep the roe that I had been pining for, but you let your brother finish it all! Don't you love me for all that I have done for both of you?'

With that, the widow went to sleep in tears. She dreamt feverishly, and in her dream, a huge rock, split and yawning, started calling for her. In the middle of the night, she got up with the voice in her head telling her to go to the rock face.

The widow hastened dreamlike out of the house, and the daughter, hearing her mother's footsteps, woke up her brother and they went in frenzied pursuit.

While running towards the rock face, the widow cried,

Batu belah, batu bertangkup, ambil aku, telan aku, aku kempunan telur tembakul!

Split rock, conjoined rock, take me, devour me, for I crave the *tembakul* roe so much!

Pausing only to leave some breast milk in a cup made of leaves for her son, the widow ran inexorably towards the now open rock face, chanting the above refrain: 'Split rock, conjoined rock, take me, devour me, for I crave the *tembakul* roe so much!' Reaching the gaping rock face, she looked back for the last time at her beloved pursuers, and dashed into the rocky maw. The rock face promptly closed, sealing the widow for ever in her stony grave.

By the time the two hapless children arrived, the rock was still and silent, betraying nothing of the tumultuous end to their mother who had just been devoured whole. Desperately prying the rock, the children realised their grieving mother was no more, buried deep behind the hard stony façade.

Second Take

JUST before the widow could throw herself into the gaping rock, the daughter cried out to her mother, '*Ibu*![1] *Ibu*! Don't do it! All the fish roe may have been eaten, but I can get some more for you! Don't do it!'

Puzzled, the mother paused before the rock face. 'What do you mean you can get some more? Don't be funny with me! I'm about to die craving for fish roe, and you want to be funny with me?' she reprimanded her daughter.

'No, *Ibu*', cried the daughter. 'Look! Look at this! Just look at this!' she continued, moving nearer to her mother. In her hand was a strange-looking object. The confused mother looked at it, and read with growing bewilderment, 'SMS message from Tesco supermarket: We are sending as per your order a one-kilogram consignment of the finest fish roe – first-class Beluga caviar specially made from Russian sturgeon.'

Crying hysterically, the mother hugged her daughter and asked, 'How did you do it?'

The triumphant daughter cooed, 'Easy, *Ibu*! With a mobile phone, I can order anything online. So will you now come home instead of doing something as irresponsible as committing suicide over fish roe? The caviar I just ordered is much better than the low-grade *tembakul* roe you wanted to die for.'

Smiling sheepishly, the mother nodded, hugging her beloved children and thankful for the marvels of modern technology. The three walked back home, and the split rock, looking hungry and stupid with its mouth gaping open, was left to endure the daughter's taunting words, 'Split rock, conjoined rock, forget it! The lady's found something far superior to *tembakul* roe. Eat your stony heart out!'

---

[1] The Malay word for 'mother'.

Bawang Putih, Bawang Merah

Bawang Putih, Bawang Merah

(Garlic and Shallot)

THE royal hunting party was deep in the forest when a melodious voice rang out clearly above the foliage.

Laju, laju, buai ku laju…

Faster, faster goes my swing…

Upon hearing it, the king could hardly contain himself. He was sure that the bewitching song was sung by a damsel who must surely be the queen of the forest. Moving quickly to the source, the entourage spotted the songstress on a swing but she disappeared into the forest just as quickly.

Completely besotted, the king ordered a search throughout his kingdom for the lady of the forest, whom he had sworn would be his bride. Word spread like wildfire throughout the land that the woman who could sing the song on the swing would be queen. Young women started to practise singing on swings, vying with each other until they grew hoarse, fully supported by their parents, and all hoping for the opportunity of a lifetime to occupy the *istana*[1] as consort to the supreme ruler.

In a house in the kingdom, two women were plotting the scheme of their lives. 'You sing the song of the damsel on the swing, and you will be queen!' shrieked the ambitious mother to her daughter, Bawang Putih. When Bawang Merah, the stepdaughter who did all the household chores and was badly treated by these two, tried to enquire into the matter, she was forthwith

---

[1] The Malay word for 'palace'.

derided. 'Look at you, ugly and smelly, how can you ever think of being the king's source of delight?'

Not too long afterwards, the royal party arrived, conducting its house-to-house search for the warbling damsel. The mother put Bawang Putih on the swing and she started to sing. The first line was enough to cause everyone to cover their ears in horror, and she was quickly ordered to stop.

When the king turned to go home in exasperation, he spotted Bawang Merah, hiding in a corner. 'Who is that?' he asked.

'That's my servant girl,' the mother replied.

'Ask her to sit on the swing!' the king ordered.

The mother protested. 'But she is only a lowly servant girl, Your Highness. How can she be the magical singer?'

Ignoring the woman, the king bade Bawang Merah to sit on the swing. There was something about her that made him doubt the mother's claim. The moment she was on it, the same melodious song issued forth, and the king was smitten for the second time. Bawang Merah was promptly married to the infatuated king. She lived happily ever after as queen of the land, forgiving her repentant stepmother and stepsister and bringing them to live with her at the *istana*.

🎬Second Take

TO THIS day, the tale of *Bawang Putih, Bawang Merah* is testimony to the ability of the Malay chanteuse to charm royalty by the sheer melody of her voice – but the story did not end there.

Bawang Merah was enjoying a blissful royal marriage when her happiness was marred by a legal notice served by solicitors on behalf of the Hollywood owner of the rights to *Cinderella*. The charge: plagiarism.

Apparently Hollywood was none too happy that *Bawang Putih, Bawang Merah*, now made into a Malay movie, had adopted its theme of a harried woman with a heart of gold, who eventually conquered all odds to emerge triumphant, yet remained magnanimous to her tormentors.

'What can I do?' Bawang Merah tearfully asked her royal hubby. 'I only sang on the swing and had no intention of hurting, let alone stealing anyone's rights. Why must I be held to account for something I don't even know about? Who is Cinderella? She does not live in my *kampung*…' And on and on she went in anguish.

'My beloved, I too am totally in the dark. When I heard your beautiful voice in the forest, my whole being was overcome with passion and emotion. I had no inkling that you had a rival by the name of Cinderella. Otherwise – '

'Otherwise what?' snapped Bawang Merah, her eyes drilling into her husband's. 'Otherwise you would choose her and not me, wouldn't you? So Cinderella sounds better than Bawang Merah? So you, like the rest of your macho ilk, would prefer a foreign name to one that is local and unglamorous? Admit it, my dear beloved husband!' she demanded, in tears.

'Oh no, my dearest Bawang Merah! You are unique. Your name, which in English means 'shallot', is far better than Cinderella or Cindy. And don't you know that your namesake is renowned for its curative properties? Why, shallot and onion have been used for generations to alleviate bronchitis and colds, and even to drive away evil spirits.'

'That's garlic, my sister Bawang Putih! Garlic is the vampire's nightmare, not shallot. But you have a point there. Bawang Merah is certainly more useful than Cinderella. Alright, all is forgiven my dear,' cooed the now placated queen.

The matter ended on a happy note when someone came up with a creative way to distinguish *Cinderella* from *Garlic and Shallot* and avoid a potential legal battle. The former involved a discarded shoe, a pumpkin carriage, and horses turned to mice. In the latter, it was just the voice in the forest, singing '*Laju laju, buai ku laju…*'

The happy ending did not quite end there. Bawang Merah was approached by recording companies and when she went on air, the world stood still. The melodious voice that had charmed the king of the land now gripped the global attention of adoring fans. Adopting a more glamorous name, Bawah Merah was now known as Charlotte, the world's most captivating songstress.

It was reported that the sale of swings drastically increased and singing schools sprouted up all over the land, attracting females of all ages, their breath reeking with onion, garlic and shallot.

Puteri Gunung Ledang

Puteri Gunung Ledang
(The Princess of Mount Ledang)

THERE once was a Malay king who ruled like a tyrant, getting whatever he wanted from his poor subjects without compunction. One day, in a dream, he saw the most beautiful and exquisite princess who hailed from Mount Ledang (a mountain somewhere in the state of Johor in southern Malaysia). The princess's enchanting beauty consumed him so much that he was prepared to do anything she wanted in order to make her his wife.

Before agreeing to marry the king, the princess asked that he fulfil several tasks to show his true love. The princess's wish list read as follows:

1. Build a bridge of gold from the *istana* right up to Mount Ledang;

2. Fill troughs with the tears of your hapless subjects;

3. Get me the hearts of mosquitoes.

'Quite easily done,' said the king, who promptly wrung the requests out of his subjects by sheer coercion. Seemingly impossible to meet, the three requests were somehow fulfilled by the heartless king who would not rest until he made the princess his wife.

To test the king's true devotion, the princess made a final request.

Get me the heart of your only son.

This was a horrible request, but the king, lovesick and blinded to reality, could see no alternative, bereft of what fatherly compassion

Puteri Gunung Ledang

he may have had. The cruel king was about to oblige, *keris*[1] drawn, when the princess suddenly appeared and berated him.

'You are a cruel man, torturing your poor subjects just to get my affection! And now you are willing to sacrifice your own flesh and blood! I wouldn't dream of having you as my partner in life, you tyrant!'

Totally heartbroken, the king eventually died a lonely and dejected man.

---

[1] A Malay curved dagger.

Second Take

HAVING lost his chance to marry the princess of his fantasy, the king somehow managed to overcome his depression and took a long flight to California. There he patented the method of super microsurgery that enabled surgeons the world over to operate even on minute life forms such as bugs and mosquitoes, thereby gaining fame and fortune and American citizenship in the land of opportunity.

However, he never stepped foot in Malaysia again, mindful of the warrant of arrest issued against him for attempted homicide of his son, and fearful of his former subjects who had now been freed and just could not wait to make him cry his eyes out for the tears they had shed into those troughs. To this day, no one knows what happened to the golden bridge from the *istana* to Mount Ledang, but for the ex-monarch, the Golden Gate Bridge of San Francisco was what mattered most in his chosen second home.

Raja Bersiong

Raja Bersiong
(The Fanged Monarch)

IN KEDAH, a northern state of Malaysia, there once lived a king who was destined to make his mark in history due to his penchant for food with a difference. His cook, in a hurry to prepare the king's favourite dish, accidentally cut his finger, causing blood to drip into the food. Not able to prepare another dish, as the king could not wait for his lunch to be served, the cook watched in trepidation as the king savoured the dish.

'Fantastic! This food is absolutely fantastic!' chimed the elated monarch. 'I want exactly the same dish tomorrow', he told the cook. The next day, the dish was duly prepared, but when he took a mouthful, the king frowned and called for the cook.

'What is this? I wanted the same cooking as yesterday, how come it is not as tasty?' The cook stammered something, and promptly rushed out of his kitchen another dish of the same ingredients, prepared to perfection.

The king took a spoonful, and spat it out. 'I want the same dish as yesterday!' he roared, 'or I'll have your head.' Thoroughly scared, the cook broke down and confessed that the other day he had cut his hand and a drop of blood was mixed with the food. Closing his eyes and expecting the worst of fate to befall him, the cook was surprised when the king ordered that blood be added to his meal each time food was prepared, and that human blood was to be made available from his subjects.

Thus it was that the crazed king indulged in his gastronomic delights, with blood extracted from his people. He soon sprouted fangs, and became known as the fanged monarch. His subjects were at first fearful but later on turned against the cruel king in rebellion. Running from the raging mob, the king tugged out his fangs and threw them far away.

Believe it or not, the place he twisted out these notorious dental protrusions is now known as Pulai (a corruption of *pulas*, meaning 'to twist'). The place after Pulai is Baling ('to throw') and after Baling, it is Siong ('fangs'), three *mukims*[1] in Kedah. The reader is invited to visit these *mukims* and talk to the locals to test the veracity of this assertion. But one thing is certain: the fanged monarch must have been a giant indeed to be able to hurl his fangs over such distances.

---

[1] The Malay word for 'district'.

Second Take

WHILE trying to escape the angry people, the king tried to pull out his fangs but could not. In desperation, he hailed a cab for Kuala Lumpur International Airport. There, he jumped on a plane to Europe where he struck up a motion picture deal. The fanged king finally found his vocation: as stand-in for Count Dracula, the Prince of Darkness.

Safely ensconced in his new career, all that Raja Bersiong needed to do was to patiently wait for the star Christopher Lee to take a break before springing in with his cloak and real fangs to perpetuate the bloody exploits of the vampire king of Transylvania. Film after film became cult box office hits but the king did not enjoy seeing his name written in the credits as simply a stand-in.

Depressed and disillusioned, the nondescript Raja Bersiong continued to indulge stealthily in his bloody repasts by visiting blood banks and volunteering as a lab assistant to take and store blood samples from donors. Somehow the deposit at the hospitals did not quite match the balance in the blood banks at the end of the day, but no one was keeping tabs and a pint or two was never missed.

Si Tanggang

Si Tanggang
(The Prodigal Son)

SI Tanggang lived with his mother in a dilapidated wooden house. From a very young age he was loved and cared for by the old woman after his father died, and the two got along famously. Si Tanggang swore to improve their lot in life and to take care of his mother in gratitude for her love and affection.

One fine day, a ship cast its anchor off the beach and Si Tanggang found the opportunity he was waiting for. Begging his mother to allow him to join the crew to sail and seek his fortune, Si Tanggang went away for the first time in his life and his tearful mother gave her blessings and prayed for his safe return.

Several years passed, and a ship cast its anchor at the same spot off the beach. Si Tanggang's mother was euphoric when told by neighbours that the captain on board was none other than her beloved son from whom she had heard nothing since he left. Beside herself with joy, she packed his favourite food, *lempeng bakar*[1], and asked to be taken out to the ship.

When the boat neared the ship, the crew informed the captain. Si Tanggang came to take a look, with a regal-looking lady by his side. Spotting her son, the mother cried,

'Tanggang! Tanggang! This is your mother! I have missed you so much, son!' Si Tanggang was bewildered and initially overcome with emotion at the sight of his old mother.

'Who is that, my dear?' asked the lady by his side.

Si Tanggang quickly regained his composure and changed his demeanour. 'Oh, no one. Just an old woman, probably looking for alms', he told his wife.

'Tanggang, don't you recognize me anymore? I'm your mother! Look, I have brought you your favourite dish, *lempeng bakar*', the mother entreated, unwrapping the food and extending it towards her

---

[1] Baked banana pancakes.

son. Embarrassed at being offered such pedestrian fare, fit only for his lowly subjects, Si Tanggang went on the defensive as his wife held tightly to him.

'Hey, old woman,' he said, 'how dare you call me 'son'? I don't even know you, and you want to offer me, a king, this thing you call food? What do you want?' he barked.

'What? Tanggang, how could you forget your own mother? You must be ashamed of my rags, and this beautiful lady must be your wife, my daughter-in-law. But I understand. Don't you remember those years of privation and struggle when you and I were so close? Remember Tanggang?' she continued hopefully, moving closer and still proffering the *lempeng bakar*.

With a contemptuous effort, Si Tanggang knocked the food away and yelled, 'Get down, you presumptuous hag! Don't you dare set foot on my ship or I will punish you! And don't you call me 'son', I don't have a mother, and even if I had one, you certainly are not her!'

Now thoroughly abused and humiliated, Si Tanggang's mother slowly made her way down to the boat, crying silently and still incredulous that her once loving son was now so hard-hearted.

'Is that your mother, my dear husband?' asked the confused lady by Si Tanggang's side.

'Not by a long shot! How can I have a tramp like that for a mother?' retorted Si Tanggang, hiding his true feelings under a layer of pretension.

As the ship set sail, Si Tanggang's mother looked up at the sky and whispered a quiet prayer to herself. 'Oh God, please show my prodigal son how wrong he was to hurt me like this'.

Without warning, the sky immediately darkened, the wind started to whip up a storm, and soon the ship was in trouble in the swirling sea.

As thunder and lightning ran amok, and just as the vessel started to capsize in the angry vortex, Si Tanggang saw his ship and crew, including his beautiful wife, turn to stone. Si Tanggang himself changed into a bird and, as he flew away, he squawked painfully in contrition: 'Forgive me, Mother, forgive me! I have sinned, I have truly sinned. Forgive me!'

It was said that the squawking bird sounded almost human in its plaintive cries. So ended the tragic tale of the prodigal son, Si Tanggang.

Second Take

THE bird park in the Lake Gardens, Kuala Lumpur, Malaysia, has one exotic species: a bird which incessantly squawks and sounds as if it were crying for its mother. The bird warden was at a loss when the bird would not eat anything, until a concerned visitor suggested it be fed *lempeng bakar*.

The warden did not notice it, but the visitor who made the suggestion had brought the pancake and had fed the bird herself, smirking in satisfaction at the sight of the grateful animal eating out of her hand. The park authorities appreciated this kind intervention and allowed the old lady to continue feeding the bird which soon became very attached to her.

She never stopped coming, until one day it was said that she had died with a smile on her ragged face. The bird pined for her and refused to eat again until it too followed suit not long afterwards, finally finding peace in its ravaged heart.

Pak Pandir

Pak Pandir

(The Imbecile)

PAK Pandir, the village imbecile, was asked to look after his infant boy by his wife who had to attend a *kenduri*[1]. She told him to be careful with the baby, and to feed and bathe him when he woke up, but only in lukewarm water. Knowing how impossibly stupid her husband was, Pak Pandir's wife showed him how to heat up the water and then how to mix it with cold water from the well so that the baby was safely bathed. She then went out, repeating her advice to her goon of a husband.

Pak Pandir settled down to sleep but was awakened by the baby's cry. Remembering his wife's reminder, he went to the kitchen and took out the milk bottle and started to feed the baby. Having done so, he decided to bathe the baby. Pak Pandir heated up the water while the baby was gurgling in the cot. When the water reached boiling point, he poured it into the basin, and took the baby in his arms. Baby looked sweetly at his father, who promptly dunked him into the hot water, killing him instantly.

Pak Pandir kept on dunking the baby, scalding his hands in the process. By the time he stopped, the baby was boiled and grinning, since the hot water had stretched his features into a ghastly smile. Pak Pandir smiled back proudly, thinking to himself that he must have done something right after all this while. He put the dead infant into the cot and covered him.

When the wife came back after the *kenduri*, Pak Pandir said he had done as he was told. His wife took one look at the baby, screamed and fainted. Pak Pandir was shocked as he thought baby's grinning face proved he had taken good care of him.

---

[1] The Malay word for 'feast'.

Second Take

IN THE dock, Pak Pandir denied he had had any intention of killing his only son as he had only wanted to give him a bath as instructed.

The deputy public prosecutor (DPP) looked at the judge, and said, 'My Lord, it is clear Pak Pandir committed cold-blooded murder of an innocent infant. He—'

But before he could finish his sentence, Pak Pandir defiantly interjected. 'Hold it! I did not commit cold-blooded murder. It was hot water, heated to boiling point. You have to prove beyond reasonable doubt that I had the *mens rea*[1] to commit homicide or manslaughter. Just because I am an imbecile does not make me a murderer!'

The judge, DPP and the rest in the gallery were stunned at this display of oratory from one thought to be of impaired mind. Finally the DPP composed himself and said, 'I will prove beyond reasonable doubt that Pak Pandir wilfully and mercilessly took his baby boy and dunked him in boiling water, killing him instantly, as he himself has just admitted doing.'

Everyone in the court strained their necks to look at Pak Pandir as he rose slowly to respond. 'My Lord,' said Pak Pandir in a clear and confident voice, 'What the honourable DPP mentioned is just the *actus reus*[2], the act of putting my son in boiling water, which I myself admit to. But where is the *mens rea*, the intention, the frame of mind of a killer? I submit, my Lord, that being in a state of diminished responsibility, I had no control of my actions, and had no inkling of what I did. Ask the village folk, ask them whether I am capable of intentionally killing my beloved son!' he implored.

'No, no… Pak Pandir is so impossibly dumb and stupid, he could never premeditate or plan, let alone actually kill anyone,

---

[1] The legal term for a premeditated intention.
[2] The legal term for the crime itself.

particularly his son whom he loved dearly', chanted the gallery, comprising nearly all the village folks who had taken time off and hired two buses to get to court.

The judge eventually dismissed the case, freeing Pak Pandir from the gallows. He was hugged by everyone, and pausing to give his thanks, Pak Pandir added, 'After this ordeal, I think I will read law and become a lawyer. With my natural abilities, I can help anyone out of any legal trouble!' he told reporters.

Unbelievably, Pak Pandir the village imbecile went on to transform himself into someone useful to society. The village soon had its famous son graduating in law, and Kuala Lumpur saw the set-up of a new law office with the name

Pak Pandir and Son (Deceased)

His speciality: tort of negligence and criminal law with special emphasis on unintentional manslaughter.

It was rumoured that Pak Pandir's consummate ability to influence the jury or judge with his arguments had convinced OJ Simpson to engage him. However he had to settle for his counsel as Pak Pandir was afraid of flying and wanted to take a ship to America instead. OJ could not afford to wait.

Si Luncai

Si Luncai

(The story of Si Luncai)

SI LUNCAI the boatman had the opportunity of his life while ferrying a boatload of robbers, with their ill-gotten gains, across the dark water of the river. He came up with a ruse.

'Look,' he said, 'the police will be here soon, and we can't get away. The only way is to let me go first with the loot. I will bury it somewhere safe and you can come to retrieve it when you have shaken them off. I'm just a boatman, and the police will never suspect me.'

The robbers looked at him suspiciously, and after some deliberation, decided to test him. 'What if you never come back or you keep it all to yourself?' they asked.

Si Luncai laughed and said, 'How can I even think of running away? You would soon have my throat cut. Listen, when the police arrive, just sing this song:

Si Luncai terjun dengan labu labunya, biarkan, biarkan!

Si Luncai jumped with his pumpkin, let it be, let it be!

With great trepidation and the utmost reluctance, the robbers passed the stolen money to Si Luncai and started to repeat the above verses.

Soon afterwards, the boat was accosted by the police who challenged it to stop. Si Luncai promptly plopped into the water. '*Si Luncai terjun dengan labu labunya, biarkan, biarkan*' sang the worried robbers. Si Luncai disappeared from the scene, never to be found.

Second Take

Sipping his lemonade, Si Luncai the millionaire looked out towards the snow-capped Alps. He had made Switzerland his second home, his money safe and sound in a Swiss account, his beautiful Swiss wife by his side.

The phone rang. Si Luncai recognized the voice. 'Sir Paul! How good to hear from you! I know how concerned you are, but I'm not going to be greedy. I have consulted my lawyers and it is very clear that I am entitled to half of the royalties. OK, I understand your feelings, but you just have to accept it. I was the one who originally composed the piece, long before your friend penned it.'

The royalties poured in from the song 'Let it be', purportedly first inspired by Si Luncai of Geneva.

Unfortunately for Si Luncai, his spurious claim landed him in hot water when he was found to have infringed copyright and the resulting lawsuit bled him dry. His Swiss wife left him in a huff, and the only thing Swiss that he had left in the end was his Swiss army knife, which he still keeps as a token of how financially blessed he once was.

Badang

Badang

(The Malay Hercules)

FRUSTRATED and nearly at his wits' end, Badang hauled up the torn net and muttered some expletives to himself. *Who the devil has done this?* he thought, fingering the fishing net that was once again shred by someone who had let out all his catch. This was the twelfth time his net had been torn and his catch stolen, and he swore that he would apprehend the thief and teach him the lesson of his life.

Badang came up with an idea. He decided to set a trap by tying a live goat to the net, and he lay in wait patiently. After half a day, he felt a tug on the net and the goat baying. Grabbing his *parang*[1], Badang sprang into the water and onto the figure struggling with the goat. It was a fearsome sight: a monster with bloodshot eyes and a horn on its forehead was starting to devour the bleating goat.

He caught hold of the figure's beard and was about to strike when it cried out, 'Don't kill me! Don't kill me! Spare me and I will reward you!'

Badang was in no mood to make any concession, remembering the numerous losses he had suffered from the torn nets, and particularly since the figure struggling to break free was so ugly and inhuman. But it was in fear of its life, and started to beg again. 'Let me go, and you will be rewarded!'

Badang loosened his grip and raising his *parang* above the creature's head, he demanded, 'What reward, you thief? You dared to steal my catch and now you want to promise me a reward?'

The demonic figure continued, 'If I am sick, will you lap up the vomit?'

Badang was violent with rage. 'What? Eat your vomit? You

---

[1] A broad Malay knife.

miserable fiend!' and he proceeded to swing the blade towards the creature's head.

'No, wait! Don't kill me! If you eat my vomit, you will acquire an awesome strength no man has ever had. Believe me!'

Badang pondered the shocking offer. Strongest man in the world by lapping up a demon's vomit? It was so incredulous yet mysteriously compelling. Some instinct told Badang not to let this chance slip by him, despite the appalling prospect of eating vomit. Dragging the creature onto dry land, Badang warned it not to run. Immediately, the creature vomited, and then made off into the forest.

Looking at the stinking sludge, Badang changed his mind and felt foolish at having been taken in so easily. But something about the creature made him think hard and, without realizing it, he soon began to lap up the gastro-excretion while straining not to vomit himself. Once done, Badang felt a fire creeping up in his belly and all over his body. Soon he was engulfed in excruciating pain, and passed out.

When he came to, Badang had a strange sensation. He felt like a new man and to his horror, found veins sprouting out from his huge arms which hung from his oak-like body. His clothing torn, Badang realized that he has been transformed physically from a weak and skinny man into a strapping, muscle-bound individual. Remembering the demon's pledge, he looked around to test his new found strength. There was a boulder by the stream. Badang went over, picked it up effortlessly, and threw it far beyond the stream as if it was a pebble. He next proceeded to uproot a tree, yanking it out with all its roots. Never before had he felt so strong and confident. Badang was now ready to conquer the world.

Soon, word spread of his amazing physical feats never performed by any other man in the land. By and by, Badang managed to curry enough favour with the local chieftain and eventually married his beautiful daughter.

Second Take

SURVEYING the range of canned powdered protein, the six-time Mr Universe proudly removed a conspicuously labelled tin from the shelf.

> Badang's Demon Puke – The hottest selling bodybuilding formula ever developed! Guaranteed to change a 100 lb sand-in-the-face weakling into a beefcake faster than you can say 'Schwarzenegger'.

Badang smiled to himself, and dreamt of the day he would occupy high political office just like his predecessor had.

★

It was the 2020 Malaysian general elections. The most talked about victor was Datuk[1] Badang who won by a spectacular margin. Soon Datuk Badang became Prime Minister, the strongest by far, and the only one who got to where he was by eating the vomit of a thieving demon.

Not satisfied and highly ambitious, Datuk Badang made a bid for the presidency of the United Nations and became the first and only Malaysian to date to occupy the Secretary General's post. (He could even have aspired to the American presidency had he wanted but, like Arnie, he was not eligible, being a foreigner).

The fairytale story of Badang ended tragically, however, when he got involved in the fight between the Shiites and occupying American forces in Iraq. Legend has it that Badang, tired of empty talk and asinine diplomacy as the UN number one, single-handedly waded into the war and scattered the American tanks before a nuclear warhead caught him in the chest.

---

[1] *Datuk* is a titled lordship conferred by royalty.

Angan Angan Mat Jenin

Angan Angan Mat Jenin
(Mat Jenin's Reverie)

MAT Jenin, or MJ, the village dreamer, could never put in a good day's work without dreaming his way through it. One day, MJ was asked to climb a coconut tree and pluck the fruits. Without batting an eyelid, he clambered up the tall tree.

Halfway through his task, he fell into his reverie.

> Once I pluck enough coconuts, I will sell them and make so much money that I will use it to buy a piece of land. I will cultivate the land and sell the produce, making more money in the process. Soon, I will be the richest man in the land! Of course, I will be able to send a delegation to the house of the *penghulu*[1] and ask for his beautiful daughter in marriage. She will never refuse the opportunity to marry a rich and handsome man like me. On our wedding day, I will put the biggest wedding ring on her dainty finger and then hold out my arms for her to come into—'

At this point MJ held out his arms, losing his grip of the coconut tree, and falling to his doom. It was a sad end to a dreamer who let his dream become his nightmare.

---

[1] Village chief.

Second Take

WHILE in free fall, MJ calmly reached below his shirt and pulled the cord. The parachute opened immediately, and he floated to the ground. Smiling as he wrapped up the chute, MJ remembered the first time it had happened when he had been saved by a passing cow that broke his fall, and also most of his bones.

Pledging never again to be caught in such a potentially mortal situation, MJ took up sky diving, eventually distinguishing himself as the first Malay BASE jumper who could do effortless routines while asleep in the air! His most memorable feat was becoming the only man to jump between the world's tallest twin towers, the Petronas Twin Towers in Kuala Lumpur.

Mat Jenin's advice to all dreamers:

> If you can dream, and not make dreams your master… you can achieve anything.

MJ's motivational books, cassettes and CDs flooded the market, local and international, and he dreamt of being the first Malay on a NASA flight to the moon. In the meantime, MJ wanted to perfect his moonwalk and develop into a thrilling singer, such was the strength of personality and self-confidence of this king of dreamers. But somehow he postponed this idea as he thought it better to devote his energies to becoming the first Malay astronaut. His pet owl would accompany MJ on his lunar flight, in defiance of the Malay proverb,

> *Bagai pungguk rindukan bulan.*

Like an owl pining for the moon, an unrequited love indeed.

Singapura di Langgar Todak

Singapura di Langgar Todak
(Singapore under Swordfish Attack)

TEMASEK, the old Singapore, was home to a gifted child called Mat who was easily the brightest spark among the Temasek denizens. Mat could solve problems that adults found too difficult to think through, and he was the most sought after person when the island had a seemingly intractable problem that needed solving.

One day, disaster hit Temasek. Schools of deadly *ikan todak*[1] started to attack the island, spearing and killing its inhabitants and creating havoc all over. The king was on the point of fleeing, when someone remembered Mat the genius boy. Mat was brought hastily to the *istana*, and to the chagrin of the palace *bomoh*[2] put forward a remarkably simple plan to save Temasek from the incessant attacks. 'Put up banana trees on the shores before nightfall', he advised.

The *bomoh* laughed at the plan, only to be told off by the desperate king. 'We have nothing to lose by listening to this boy, but everything to gain if it works. Get it done!' barked the king.

The entire population set upon the task of cutting down banana trees and hauling the banana trunks to the shores of the island. Before nightfall, the shores were secured by rows upon rows of banana trunks. The shaman again pooh poohed the effort, saying that Temasek would suffer even more by partaking of this crazy scheme thought up by a boy.

The next day, very early in the morning, a cry rang out across the island. 'Look! Look! It worked! It worked!'

Everybody, the king included, rushed to the shores, and lo and

---

[1] Swordfish.
[2] A shaman, someone regarded as having influence in the world of good and evil spirits.

behold, before their incredulous eyes, they saw hundreds of struggling swordfish with their snouts stuck upon the banana trunks. The joyous people proceeded to hack and slash the evil fish and Temasek became peaceful once again. Mat the genius boy was heralded as a hero and was rewarded handsomely by the grateful king.

However, the *bomoh* did not rest until he could hatch up a plot to make the king turn against the boy. Whispering into the monarch's ear, he warned that if Mat could think up such a scheme at his age, what kind of a threat would he pose to the palace when he grew up? Ambition and genius were a dangerous combination. The worried king now got to thinking about his future, and agreed with the *bomoh* that the boy could not be allowed to live.

Thus Mat the genius boy was executed for being too smart and for fear that he may grow up ambitious and hungry for power. Temasek did not remain peaceful for long, as the *ikan todak* made a more deadly return, descending on the island like arrows and impaling the *bomoh*, the king and all his subjects.

🎬Second Take

MAT, being the genius that he was, quickly thought up a plan to stay alive and well when he sensed that the *bomoh* could easily influence the king. Making his way to the *istana* at night, he managed to get to the king when the *bomoh* was not in.

Mat hastened to advance his plan thus, 'O King, I know I have made you happy by ridding Temasek of the *ikan todak*. Now, I want to make you happier'.

Puzzled, the king asked how he could be made happier. Putting his mouth to the king's ear, Mat whispered, and the king's eyes grew wide in excitement.

★

The Royal Satay & Swordfish Steak House opened for business in downtown Temasek, occupying a corner lot in what is now Shenton Way. It was a riot from the start, attracting local and foreign tourists, and its main draw was the flying *todak* steak on banana leaf.

The partnership yielded such a rich stream of revenue for the king and Mat that they decided to franchise the business. By the time Temasek became Singapore, there were close to 10,000 outlets throughout Asia and Europe, with a new outlet to be opened in New York in 2006 after its successful launches in London, Paris and Tokyo. Even Starbucks did not come close in terms of business volume and profit.

And the *bomoh*? He was exiled to Pulau Batu Putih where he worked as the lighthouse keeper, and died a lonely man long before the rocky island became a disputed territory.

Postscript

*M*ALAY *folklore continues to captivate and enthral through modern mediums such as the cinema and television. Malays are aware these tales are the product of the imagination of their ancestors, but could not abandon their association with the tales. In the above retelling, many liberties were taken and quite understandably, some may have taken umbrage.*

To these purists – take heart that the retelling may have the effect of introducing local lore to the world. In today's global village, why not tell people about our own Pak Pandir after hearing about Mr Bean? Why just gape at Dracula when we have our own Raja Bersiong? And why wonder at the Dutch boy who saved Holland from the floods when we have our boy genius of Temasek fame? Superman is strong, but surely no match for Badang, and should we not also be proud of our Bawang Putih, so far ahead of Cinderella? Even the Loch Ness monster of Scotland has its local equivalent in Naga Tasik Cini (the equally elusive dragon of Cini Lake in Pahang on the east coast of Malaysia).

Malay Folklore will remain just that: lore to be enjoyed by generations who needed reminding that, despite the frantic pace of life and the generational gaps between grandparents and their grandchildren, a little bit of far-fetched oral tradition is a welcome and nostalgic respite, regardless of its occasional non sequitur. And no one holds a stranglehold on the exact correctness of its storyline, save purists who may want to cling on to images created through posterity. We take full responsibility for the parodies here as we believe a contemporary retelling with a twist may evoke some interest in the modern youth excessively caught up in gadgetry and electronics.

Printed in Great Britain
by Amazon